For Holly Jones-Warren,
with love
I.W.

For Lottie,
and with thanks to Kate
D.M.

Jump in!

Ian Whybrow

David Melling

Hodder
Children's
Books

A division of Hodder Headline Limited

British Library Cataloguing in Publication Data
A catalogue record of this book is available from the British Library

ISBN 0 340 739908 (PB)

Text copyright © Ian Whybrow 1999
Illustrations copyright © David Melling 1999

The right of Ian Whybrow to be identified as author
of this Work and of David Melling as illustrator of this Work
has been asserted by them in accordance
with the Copyright, Designs and Patents Act 1988

First published in 1999
by Hodder Children's Books,
a division of Hodder Headline Limited,
338 Euston Road, London NW1 3BH

1 0   9

Printed in Hong Kong

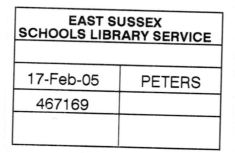

Miss Lollipop was lonely, so
She bought a little truck.
She drove down to the river -
And in jumped . . .

. . . a duck!

'How lovely!' said Miss Lollipop,
'I was all alone before.
But I'm very fond of animals.
Let's go and find some more!'

The little duck went
Quack-quack-quack!
And the truck went
Beep-beep-beep!
They stopped for a little picnic
And in jumped . . .

. . . a sheep!

The duck went quack
The sheep went baaaa!
Miss Lollipop said, 'That's nice!'
She drove them to a mousehole
And in jumped . . .

. . . two mice!

Off they went with a

Quack-baaa-squeak!

Miss Lollipop said,

'Where now?'

The little mice said,

'Cowshed, please!'

And in jumped . . .

Cowshed

. . . a cow!

The cow said, 'Moo!
Let's go to the zoo!'
Miss Lollipop gave a laugh.
And in jumped a kangaroo,
And a very tall . . .

... giraffe!

The poor giraffe was homesick
And missed the sunshine so,
That Miss Lollipop drove to Africa
And found . . .

. . . a buffalo!

The buffalo said a rough, 'Hello!'
Then he said, 'Oh, what a lot of us!'
Miss Lollipop said, 'Yes, quite a few,
But there's room for · · ·

. . . a hippopotamus!

The hippo sighed, 'I'd love a ride,
But sadly I'm not thin, dear.'
Miss Lollipop said, 'Don't fuss, jump in!'
Then off she drove to India.

India

Miss Lollipop called out,
'Squeeze up, please!'
The animals cried, 'We can't!'
'There's no more room on board this truck!
Oh no! It's . . .

. . . an ELEPHANT!'

Just then a tiger came along
And he grinned his tiger grin.
He opened up his tiger mouth
And the tiger said . . .

'. . . JUMP IN!'

Miss Lollipop said, 'You naughty boy!'
And she chased him in her truck.
For inside the tiger's tummy was . . .

1 elephant

1 buffalo

1 hippopotamus

1 giraffe

1 cow

2 little mice

1 sheep

1 kangaroo

1 duck!

Then the tiger got the hiccups,
And they popped out one by one.

Miss Lollipop said, 'Was that horrid for you?'
But the animals said . . .

So the very next morning, can you believe,
Although it had started to rain,
Along came Miss Lollipop in her truck
And . . .

. . . they all jumped in again!

How many animals did Miss Lollipop find?
Can you go back and count them all again?

The End